BLURB

Shibari Khaleej– Genie
Lead Female Character – Bianca
Ebony Grey
Grandmother – Katrina Grey
Mustafa – The Kings Sorcerer
King – Mohammad bin Al Saud

* * *

Once upon a time, long ago when tales of Ali Baba and the Forty Thieves were bedtime stories and *Scheherazade* was titled Queen of 1001 tales in 1000 nights, there was a Prince who dared to wish for something more than a kingship.

When Bianca Ebony Grey was just a little girl, she was taken in by her grandmother Katrina Grey, after both of her parents were killed in an automobile accident. She was raised with love and affection, but no matter how old she got, whether it be six, twelve or twenty-five she was forbidden to touch the ancient Arabian teapot. Until eventually her grandmother passed away and Bianca was forced to pack up her house.

Biting her lip in trepidation, she reaches up onto her tip-toes to takes ownership of her grandmother's most prized possession. Studying the intricate patterns adorning the creation she turns it this way then that as she whispers to herself.

"I wish I understood why Grandma Grey forbid me to touch you?"

Bianca gasped as the teapot heated and steam began to pour out of the spout. She then choked on her gasp as a half-naked man appeared and demanded to know, "Who dares to summon Shibari?"

RUB ME THE RIGHT WAY

A PARANORMAL ROMANCE NOVELLA

MELISSA BELL

CONTENT WARNING

The following eBooks contains Adult (18+) Themes, including graphic sexual scenes and language as well as drug references which may offend or disturb some readers. All characters are fictional and portrayed as mature adults 18 years old and over.

DEDICATION

*I dedicate this novella to two awesome authors
who inspire me.
Because of them I dream big, I wish hard and
I'm not going home without both titles
- New York Times & USA Today Best Sellers -
One Down and One To Go.*

LAURANN DOHNER

*You are truly my favourite author and one day I
hope to be
as brilliant as you.*

&

S. E. Smith
(Susan E. Smith)
*It was a pleasure meeting you at the
Riveting Read Author Signing
in Brisbane – Australia 2017.
You showed me that commitment
and determination can keep you on the path.*

ACKNOWLEDGMENTS

~ JORDIN THIELE ~

Thank you!
I would not be able to do what I do, without
you.
Love Always

PROLOGUE

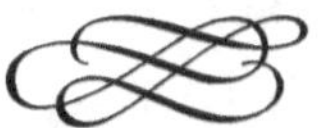

Once upon a time, long long ago when tales of Ali Baba and the Forty Thieves were bedtime stories and Scheherazade was made Queen of 1001 tales in 1000 nights. There was a Prince who dared to wish for something more.

* * *

"I HEAR the hollowness of your words Prince Shibari. You dishonour your title and shame my name. So, for this crime, you will forever be trapped by your wishes." King Mohammad bin Al Saud cursed Prince Shibari, and in doing so gave his sorcerer on staff the permissions he needed to carry out the King's decree. After all, it was only a fool who would decline the hand of the Kings second daughter.

That evening as Prince Shibari prepared to travel to the neighbouring city of Medina to continue his search for true love. He shook his head at the belief of the old kings in joining hands for the sake of convenience and lands. Shibari refused to accept his fate for anything less than love.

He wished to find a wife who would gladly beg to be bedded by him every night. Prince Shibari would not rule his house in the same manner of his forefathers by growing a harem fifty or one hundred strong at the risk of breaking the heart of his one true love.

The Prince was so certain of his beliefs that true love actually existed, that it was what had persuaded him to search the vast lands and many cities for that one special female to call his own. He knew in his heart, that if he found her, he would have no desire to be with another and they would have a house filled with love for each other and that love would grow between them to produce well-loved children. Those children would know the bounds of his love for their mother, as she would be the only woman permitted to enter his bed.

A knock at the door caused Prince Shibari to pause in packing his saddlebags. A warning sensation raised the hairs on the back of his neck. Uncertain of whether it was his father's men who had come to take him home, or someone else who wished to bargain for the life of a Prince and the future King of Mecca. So, he unlatched the door cautiously with one hand on his dagger.

"Apologies for the disturbance Sire. My father requested that I bring you some food and drink before the sun sets." Keisha the innkeeper's daughter bowed graciously while holding a tray of bread, cheeses, and water. Prince Shibari relaxed his hand on his blade and stepped back to open the door to his room, ready to gesture towards the small table by the window. The clatter of plates and cups hitting the stone floor gave cause for Shibari to look back in Keisha's direction to find a group of heathens had made their way to his quarters. The young Keisha's hair was wrapped around the fist of a barbaric male and his bloodstained blade was pressed against her neck.

"You will drop your blade Prince Shibari or I will slice the girls throat," Abba demanded.

As Prince Shibari tossed his dagger to the ground in surrender, "Who sent you?" Shibari commanded. The Prince knew they were mercenaries and that it made no difference who the coin was coming from, it was simply about the number of gold pieces they would be paid.

"I will give you a thousand pieces if you simply walk away now and tell your master you did not find me," Shibari offered.

"Faruk and Abdul take him before the fool insults us further with his meagre barter." Abba directed his men to take hold of the prince.

Shibari did not fight as Abba still had hold of the young Keisha, and he believed the threat to her was very much as real as the words Abba had spoken.

"The deal we have struck with Mustafa Chukarah the king's sorcerer cannot be broken. It has been sworn in blood, you are worth your weight in gold. Besides, nobody crosses Mustafa and lives to tell about it." Abba walked up to Shibari and fisted his hair, and with a snap of his fingers under the Prince's nose an ampule was broken, and the last thing Shibari saw was Keisha impaled on a blade at the hand of one of the mercenaries who had not yet entered the room.

Faiz wiped his blade on the females smock then threaded it through the sash that was tied around his waist to hold it in place. "I will get the horses," he said as he moved towards the front of the inn.

Within the hour Prince Shibari had been delivered to the king's sorcerer. Shibari slowly woke to find his hands and feet had been bound. His skin felt as though it were on fire and his throat was so parched that when his lips moved not a single word came out.

Mustafa lifted a cup to the sky and lightning struck with a sizzle. The king's sorcerer chanted well into the night, during which time Shibari floated in and out of consciousness. Each time, his life flashed before his eyes. In his semi-conscious state, he recognised those images for what they represented, his dreams for the future. They were his wishes and the sorcerer was taking them from him, turning them against him. No matter how hard Shibari tried to fight the outcome, it was sadly inevitable. And when blackness overtook him, he felt his essence slowly leave his physical body.

Shibari regained consciousness a small handful of times, but each time was only to sink deeper into an overwhelming desperation. He failed to understand what had, in fact happened to him. One of the many questions he had, was to know if the sorcerer had taken away his sight, as he was constantly surrounded by darkness. The circular room he was being held in, had no doors that he could find and the strange thing was, that the room appeared to move in a strange rocking manner. Finally giving in to his captivity he sat down in the middle of the room with his legs crossed and waited, after all, patients was one of his strong suits.

Shibari must have fallen asleep, for which he chastised himself for when a small amount of light filtered in through a strange grid in the wall of his prison. As he prepared to fight whoever was outside his confines, he felt his enclosure heat up.

Mustafa stood before his king and presented the golden Arabian teapot. King Mohammad bin Al Saud accepted the gift turning it sideways when he was about to pass it to one of his guards, Mustafa cried out, "No! Master, I beg your pardon but I present you with your enemy. My King, if you rub the teapot the genie will appear and provide you with three wishes. I thought it a suitable gift to present in exchange for your daughter's hand in marriage. Mustafa bowed to express his willingness to serve the king. The king raised his eyebrow at the man who dared to lay claim to his daughter of royal breeding. So, with barely a nod of his head, he rubbed the side of teapot until a great puff of smoke appeared to ooze from the spout. As the air cleared the king recognised the face of Prince Shibari. He turned to Mustafa and asked, "What is the meaning of this? This trickery is of evil-doing, and I will not have any of it in my house. I wish you banished from my lands by sea."

Without being able to stop the words from forming on his lips, Shibari uncrossed his arms, clapped twice and replied, "As you wish." Within the blink of an eye, Mustafa vanished from the king's sight and was placed on a raft in the middle of the Arabian Sea.

The king horrified by his own wishes forbid anyone to touch the teapot, therefore after wishing the genie to go back into his housing, the king sneaked down into the unground caverns and buried it. And that's where it stayed for the next seven years until the king's grandson ran down to the catacombs trying to hide from his tutor. Young Binu in his juvenile awkwardness tripped over as he glanced back over his shoulder while running. Scampering into the shadows he sat on a small mound of dirt only to be prodded in the posterior by the handle of an Arabian teapot. Tugging it free he toppled back as his tutor's hand closed on his shoulder. Binu rubbed the teapot on the sleeve of his tunic eager to clean up his find. The pot heated up and Binu almost dropped it when vapour began to pour from the spout.

"Who summons Shibari?" The genie asked emerging from the mist.

The tutor fell to his knees and started to pray, but Binu was far more brazen than smart. His chest puffed up and the king's grandson admitted, "It was I, Prince Binu Mohammed Al Saud."

"Very well Prince Binu Mohammed Al Saud. I will grant you three wishes." The genie offered the young boy.

"I wish I was all growed up." Binu made his first wish.

Shibari unfolded his arms, bowed his head and replied. "Your wish is my command." He clapped twice and the child Binu burst the seems of his tunic as he grew and grew, ageing twelve years in a matter of minutes.

Prince Binu lifted his hands to feel his chest and abdominal muscles noting that he was a very fit male. He then touched his face and established that he was old enough to have facial hair and the length of the hair on his head was down past the middle of his back. The smile quickly faded from the young man as his body began to wither and age at a rapid rate.

"Stop!" Binu Cried, "I only wanted to be older. I did not want to be old."

"My apologies Prince Binu but you were not specific as to an age you wished to be." Shibari folded his arms to ward off any argument. He had surrendered to his fate and in doing so, had given up some of his heart and mind. Loneliness had driven him a smidgen off balance, and he chose to twist the wishes into what he believed to have heard, not what they necessarily intended. Pan faced, he tilted his head to the side, "If you have a particular age you wish to be, then you will need to request it and I shall grant it to you as your second wish."

"I want to be twenty-five," the quickly ageing Binu said.

Shibari yarned hiding his mouth with the back of his hand to indicate boredom if he continued to stall the young prince would be dead within the next five minutes from old age. "You will need to be more direct. What you want and what you wish for are two totally different things in this instance."

"I wish to be twenty-five!" Binu rushed the words out as his legs threatened to give way.

"Your second wish is my command," Shibari clapped twice and Binu inhaled a sigh of relief as the ageing process reversed and then stopped. "That is two wishes young prince, which leaves you with just one more."

"I wish to be as learned as him," Prince Binu pointed at his tutor.

"I grant your third and final wish." Shibari clapped once, "Your wish is my command," he then clapped a second time before bowing to Prince Binu. As Prince Binu bowed and stood back up, the genie was gone and a trail of mist slithered back into the spout of the teapot and the pot spun in three times then disappeared from sight.

Prince Binu was feeling very proud of himself walking up the steps into the palace only to have the guards cross their spears before him, blocking him from re-entering the main palace.

"What is the meaning of this? I am Prince Binu Mohammed Al Saud and you will allow me to pass."

The guards looked at one another uncertain of what to make of the young man's decree. Impatient to clear things up Prince Binu demanded, "Take me to my grandfather now!"

"Arrest this imposter," the leader of the guards commanded.

"I will see you flogged and hanged for this," Prince Binu yelled as the guards did as their leader bid them to do. "I demand you take me to my grandfather the king now!"

"The king of whom you refer is dead, he died many years ago of a broken heart when his grandson disappeared. He was a boy of only six."

Prince Binu shook his head in disbelief, "No that can't be. I only went down to the catacombs this morning. My tutor was with me, find him. Ask him, he will tell you of what he saw. Who rules the palace if the king is dead?"

"King Hassam, second grandson to King Mohammad bin Al Saud," the leader of the guard informed him.

CHAPTER 1

s the sun set in the city of Medina the teapot shone brightly in the window of the House of Hassam. When the King entered his bedroom to get changed for dinner, the light hit the edge of it catching his eye. He frowned at the object which had appeared from nowhere, and tried to recall ever seeing it in his chambers before. Finally, he had to admit that he had not previously laid eyes on it.

The closer he stepped towards the teapot the brighter the reflection of the sun bounced off of its surface. It was so intense that as he drew near enough to pick it up he almost knocked it off the window ledge.

Finally, with the teapot in his grasp, he moved away from the window and sat on the floor to study the intricate designs on the outside of the Arabian teapot. He opened his palm face up and tilted the teapot to see if there was anything inside it to account for the unusual weight of it. He waited and watched for even a droplet but there was nothing. He attempted to remove the lid, he twisted it sideways then upside down, but nothing seemed to budge the lid or break the seal between the top and the bottom. Finally giving up on wasting any-more of his time on something so trivial, he tossed the teapot aside. Pushing himself back up off the floor cushions he straight-ened his tunic, tugged at his sleeves and lifted his head. The instant he did, he was blinded by the glare of the teapot sitting on the window ledge shining in the last rays of the afternoon sun.

The king thinking someone was playing tricks on him, turned in a full circle to verify if he was in his chamber alone or if one of his concubines had entered his quar-ters, but the room was empty of any other occupants. He turned his gaze back towards the teapot and with determination, he stomped to where it sat proudly and pushed it off the ledge. The king leaned out the window to observe it falling towards the ground, he clapped his hand as though dusting off dirt or dust and decided to visit with his mistresses to take his mind off the unusual events of the afternoon.

The king spent many hours being bathed, fed and pampered by the women in the House of Hassam's harem. Finally, with a full belly and a sated cock he returned to his quarters to retire for the night. As he entered his bedding room the bright light of the full moon bounced off a shiny surface on the other side of his chambers, catching his attention. As he moved further into his room he held his breath and he drew closer to the window. Much to his horror, the Arabian teapot sat on the window ledge the same as it had earlier that day only moments prior to the king pitching off the ledge down to the ground outside. He'd seen it with his own eyes. Confused he wondered at the oddity of how the object kept returning to his line of sight. Opting to ignore it he disrobed and climbed into bed, turning his back on the irritating item he fell into a deep sleep.

In the early hours of the morning at the end of a rather juicy dream, King Hassam rolled over to his other side. Eventually, he woke to stare at the teapot still resting on the window ledge. Mumbling to himself he left the comfort of his bed and approached the teapot. Finally, after observing it for a number of minutes, he chose to take a closer look at the intricate patterns adorning the pot. As he turned it this way and that investigating every curl of work-manship, he had to admit that it was like none he had ever seen before. As his thumb gently rubbed back and forth on the side of it, he muttered to himself. "I wish I knew what was inside of you that is so weighted?" He held the handle by a threaded finger and the base balanced on the palm of his other hand. The exasperated gasp sounded loud even to the king's ears as the teapot heated and steam began to pour from the spout.

"Who summons Shibari?" the genie

asked as his feet settled on the Persian carpet covering the floor. He folded his arm and tilted his head inspecting his surroundings.

"I... I..." Hassam responded with a loss for words.

"Never mind." Shibari waved his hand at the stuttering king as he ceremoniously sat on the collection of cushions on the floor. Crossing his legs, he pinched his middle finger and thumb together on each hand, then rested the backs of both hands on a knee each. "I am here to grant you three wishes. However, you have used one of the wishes to get me here so that technically only leaves two."

King Hassam glanced around the room then settled on the floor opposite the genie, "So in your experience, what sort of things do people wish for?"

Shibari felt a stab to his heart, "I know if I had the privilege of making a wish then I would choose something that I feel I cannot live without." The genie explained not wanting to give any more of himself away. He'd already had everything else stolen from him, whatever was left was his and his alone.

King Hassam rubbed his hands together and looked around his room before asking in words barely loud enough to hear over a whisper, "I wish to have a manhood that is enough to satisfy every single woman in my harem." Hassam held up his hands provided a visual of what he thought would be ample.

Shibari studies the dimension and then with a nod of his head he lifted his hands and clapped three times, "Your wish is my command."

Hassam watched as his cock grew to match his wish. Ecstatic with the results of his wish he stood and sashayed around the room. The weight of his much larger shaft gave him pause, with his feet planted in the one spot he swivelled his hips from side to side and watched with self-appraisal as his cock bounced from the top of one thigh to the other and back again. The smile on his face grew with each slapping sound.

Satisfied with his second wish king Hassam contemplated his third and final wish. "I have as much money and power as

I'll ever want. However, I do not have an heir to my throne, therefore, I believe it is time that I take a bride. In saying this I would wish for the most beautiful wife in all the lands."

Shibari tilted his head to the side, closed his eyes briefly and then ever so slowly opened his eyes once again. His hands came up next to his tilted head and he clapped them thrice, "Your wish is my command."

The young woman who appeared in the middle of the room was the most stunning female the king had ever seen. He bowed to her immediately and asked for her hand in marriage.

Jasminda blinked several times as though she were in a dream, "I… Um… I'm sorry my king I do not understand what you ask of me."

"I want to marry you and make you my queen." King Hassam explained.

Jasminda almost fainted with surprise, "I do not know what to say."

"Just say yes." King Hassam persuaded. "Tell her to say yes." He turned expecting to see the genie still in the room but there was nobody but the woman he planned to make his wife and himself.

Shibari had vanished back into his teapot as the third and final wish settled on his ears. The tail of smoke was sucked back into Shibari's prison as it spun three times and then disappeared.

After trying to explain her circumstances to the king who was not willing to listen, Jasminda agreed to Hassam's proposal. Averting her eyes from the king's nudity, she sat on the cushions on the floor as the king went about waking up the entire house to announce that the House of Hassam had found their Queen and that they had a wedding to prepare for.

Word spread throughout the palace like wildfire and within a short time the women of the House of Hassam's Harem began to look for information and answers but their slave girl was nowhere to be found.

For all the years that Jasminda had worked within the palace walls, nobody had ever taken the time to ask for her name. When they did refer to her they simply called out 'Girl' and Jasminda responded without introductions or corrections. She had never once looked directly at them, because someone of her station was not worthy of laying eyes on the likes of royalty. They were not spoken to unless it was to fetch something or do something for one of the women.

Jasminda was given her own room and was well provided for. Two of the eunuchs from the harem carried in a large tub and then proceeded to fill it with heated water and oil pressed from rose petals. The taller of the two slid a sideways glance at Jasminda, frowned but then shook his head as though his thoughts were not true. Regardless, the king was more particular about the males who stood guard over his harem. When their manhood was taken so was their tongues. This was to prevent tales being released outside the sanctity of the harem and prevented them from passing on secrets about the inner workings of the palace. As Habeeb closed the doors to Jasminda's chamber, he turned to her, lifted his finger to his lips to indicate that he would remain silent of her identity. When her eyebrows lifted and her eyes widened, Habeeb bowed at her with a glimmer in his eyes before closing the doors securely.

When Jasminda removed her clothing, and slid into the warmth of the tub she turned to the stool sitting beside the bath. Perched to one side of the stool were a sea sponge and a small bottle of oil. To the other side was a teapot, Jasminda puzzled at what it was doing on the stool, as there was nothing to drink tea from.

Jasminda was unbelievably drawn to the swirls, scalloping, and leafing, it was spellbinding in its beauty. Unable to take her eyes off it, she lifted her left hand and ran her pointed index finger along the edge of the filigree from the tip of the spout to the curl of the handle. As she withdrew her touch the teapot heated and steam began to pour from the spout in a pattern that went over the edge of the stool and towards the floor. Jasminda thought that very peculiar as steam normally rose not sank. She squeaked as the mist cleared and a male stood in its place.

"Who dares to summon Shibari?"

"I… I…" the young female offered as her right hand lifted to touch the back of her head, appearing as though she thought she may have bumped it. However, before her fingers could make it to her hair, she fainted.

Shibari sighed, unfolding his arms he clicked his fingers in exasperation, and the soon to be queen was deposited into her bed a breath before he disappeared back into his prison. When Jasminda was woken a couple of hours later by the wrapping of knuckles on the door she sat up in bed to discover she was clothed and no longer in the bath. Confusion crossed her beautiful face until she spied the Arabian teapot on the nightstand beside her.

She raced for the door to open it quickly not wanting to be alone with the cursed item. Jasminda was bombarded by a flock of females who took over her care. Her hair was quickly bound and decorated with ornaments suitable for a queen. Her wedding gown was laid out on the bed along with a pair of slippers. They applied henna to the backs of her hands and around her wrists.

The gems that hung like tiny teardrops in the center of her forehead were stunning.

Jasminda felt pushed this way and that until finally everyone took a step away from their future Queen. If Hassam thought her beautiful when he'd first seen her, then he was sure to believe her a goddess upon catching sight of her now.

Jasminda paced anxiously back and forth, praying that Hassam would come to visit her before they were to commit to each other. She turned to look out the window to see the Arabian teapot on the ledge. Biting her lower lip, she walked over to where she could take a closer look at it. Using her left hand, she picked it up by the handle and studied the swirls and curls rubbing her fingertips over the bumps she whispered to herself, "I wish I knew what to do."

As the words left her lips the teapot began to heat and steam poured from the spout, the mist forming a masculine shape until the deep voice of Shibari spoke, "Who dares to summon Shibari?"

"My name is Jasminda," she took a step

backward. "And I did not call for you, so be gone."

"Ha! You know not what you speak." Shibari crossed his arms defiantly at being dismissed by the female. He raised an eyebrow with curiosity to see what the wishes of a woman would be like compared to those of a male. He wondered if females would want larger chests, skinnier waists and smaller feet. Never mind he concluded they were all the same, greedy. "You wished you knew what to do. So, I will count that as the first of your three wishes."

"I need to know what to do. I am but a servant girl who works for the women of the House of Hassam. What if they recognize me? The king will have me killed for disgracing his name."

"Have no fear Jasminda, you are exactly what the king wished for. He wanted the most beautiful woman to take as his queen. If he ever should discover the truth then you should know he did not wish for a beautiful woman who possessed royal blood. He did not wish for a beautiful woman worth her weight in gold. He simply asked for the most beautiful woman in all the lands. Therefore, you will marry the king and become his queen and provide him with his heir to the throne. He will be so in love with your true beauty, both inside and out that he will no longer have a need for the women in the House of Hassam's Harem and they will be returned to where they came from with a tidy purse of gold and their freedom to find their own husbands."

"Thank you, Shibari," Jasminda replied feeling relief with the genie's prophecy.

"Yes, well, I don't have all day." Shibari clicked his fingers impatiently. "Next wish? You have two remaining, what shall they be?"

"Can I ask a question?" Jasminda asked cautiously.

"Yes, if you must." The genie sighed.

"What would you wish for if I were to be the one granting your wishes?" She said, lifting her chin with a show of courage that she truly didn't possess.

"I wish I was free to find someone who will love me for me not for what I can give them. I would also wish that if I found such a love the spell that commands me would be broken forever."

Jasminda smiled shyly as she prepared to speak. "I wish Shibari could find a true love strong enough to break the spell which binds him to his prison."

Shibari's legs shook at what he'd heard, "I do not understand why you would use one of your wishes on me. Is this really what you wish for?"

Jasminda nodded her head to indicate that she was certain of her words. Shibari bowed his head in respect for the future queen then clapping his hands he spoke, "Your wish is my command," Shibari's words were slightly choked as he tried to maintain control over his emotions. For the first time, Shibari had something to cling to... Hope.

* * *

SADLY, for Shibari, his wish did not come true from one century to the next, and he was convinced that he would never be free.

When his mind became bitter and twisted he reminded himself of Jasminda's wish for him. It may not have come true, but there was still hope that one day he would meet another like King Hassam's Queen.

CHAPTER 2

H ere and now...

BIANCA EBONY GREY sat with her head down and her eyes focused on her white handkerchief edged with lace. She fingered the corner where her grandmother had embroidered her initials.

She reframed from looking up at the most influential person in her entire life, the person who was presently surrounded by flowers. It was too painful to admit that her larger than life Grandmother, Katrina Grey fitted into that tiny coffin. Bianca bit her lower lip knowing that her grandmother's favourite hat would have taken up more room than what the tinderbox offered.

A tear escaped the corner of her eye as she faced the cold hard truth that she had no family left. Grandma Grey had taken her in after her parents had both been killed by a drunk driver. She rubbed the lettering again as a reminder of how lucky she was to be alive. Even the doctors had whispered about miracles, prayers, and wishes but grandma Grey had not left her side the whole time she had been in an induced coma while her body healed from all the trauma. Except for the physical scars Bianca honestly didn't remember that night and she probably never would. Sometimes she thought she saw flashes but every time she tried to grasp onto the images within her dreams they would morph and change.

Up until a couple of days ago, she had still planned to take time off from her busy schedule to visit with her grandmother. The visits had become increasingly less frequent due to the fact that every time Nana Grey knew she was planning to visit, it seemed

that every eligible male in the area coinci-
dently came knocking on her grandmother's door. The last one had been creepier
than all get out, Bianca hiccupped as she
tried to stop herself from laughing at the
fact that the man now standing at the front
of the church was the same man that had
come calling. The only difference was that
he now wore a suit and was part of the funeral package her grandmother had pur-
chased. Although Grandma Grey was still
quite active in the community she had
grown more and more forgetful with age.
Bianca was surprised that she'd lived as long
as she had considering her allergies. Normally she never left the house without her
epi-pen, but when a young single man
moved into the house next door, Katrina
had taken an interest in finding out if he
would be interested in meeting her granddaughter Bianca. She'd carried over the
chicken pot pie ready to present it as a
means of breaking the ice with the young
man. As her foot hit the second to last step,
her free hand brushed the banister housing
a swarming wasp's nest. She was attacked

viciously and was stung multiple times on her hand, face, and neck. Within seconds her throat began to close and she was unable to breathe. When the pie dish hit the veranda making an explosive sound and the door flew open, it was already too late to save Katrina Grey.

Bianca had met her grandmother's new neighbour and almost laughed at the irony of the situation. If her grandmother hadn't been trying to set her up with Andrew, she wouldn't have been placed in a position to pay with her life that day. The price of finding out that Andrew was indeed single, but that was only because he'd caught his boyfriend Barry cheating on him with Sanjai.

Andrew had come to visit the night Bianca had arrived to take care of her grandmother's arrangements. Within just a short time of her being in the small coastal town of Sunshine people had started to converge on her sanctuary. Including the man who now read the eulogy. Franklyn Moon had been courting her grandmother for over five years. He'd given Katrina one year's grace after Bianca's grandfather passed away then he'd made his move.

Numb, that pretty much covered it. Bianca felt completely numb from head to toe, except for the fact that it hurt to breath she couldn't feel a thing. She closed her eyes as she tried to block out the sounds of others chattering and whispering around her. Nope, she concluded there wasn't one breath that hurt more than the other – breathing in and out hurt equally. As her toes pinched into her black heels she heard Mavis Peacock utter to Sonia Castle, "I wonder if Bianca will let me have a peek at Katrina's…" the sentence was never finished as Bianca stood and pulled her shoes off in front of everyone before pitching them one at a time towards the two old ladies sitting at the other end of the row behind her, as she did so she screamed, "Fuck off you pair of old crows. My grandma isn't even ashes yet and you're already wondering if you can get your hands on her prize-winning recipes. Seriously get out!" Bianca put her hands on her hips and stood her ground. "In fact, all of you get out. You old buzzards can circle the 'For Sale Sign' a week from now. Until then have some respect, she didn't like any of you two-faced knob jockey's any more than you liked her. Unless you needed help fundraising for some hopeless charity, like putting a new steeple on this god-awful hovel you call a church she never even heard from you from one week to the next." Bianca's sacrilegious mouthful created a roomful of horrified gasps. Finally, when nobody moved to exit the chapel, Bianca stomped out the front door and over to where she had parked her car.

Bianca couldn't care less that the sky took that moment to open up the heavens and rain down on her parade. She pulled her keys from her shoulder bag and pressed the button to unlock the car, "Fabulous!" she exclaimed as the remote access failed to unlock it. Shaking her head in frustration she used the key to open the door and sank heavily into the driver's seat. Johnathon Hardie held the door open stopping Bianca from shutting it. "Still running away, I see," Johnathon pointed out in the smug fashion he was well known for.

"Still chasing tail, I see," Bianca retorted sarcastically knowing that Johnathon had been trying to get into her panties since the ninth grade.

Johnathon squatted down next to Bianca, one hand fell to her knee and the other held the umbrella above the gap between the car and the door. "Why don't I follow you home, I don't think you should be alone right now."

Bianca's jaw dropped as she mentally shook herself to verify she'd just heard this douche as he focused on nailing her. Sure, her makeup was running down her face and she probably looked like an extra from 'Fright Night' but for fuck sake, there was something seriously wrong with the entire population of Sunshine. Johnathon took Bianca's silence as a green light and started to move his hand toward the intersection between her legs. The Brush of his knuckles against the inside of her thigh brought her slamming back to reality with a jolt. Her hand grabbed his wrist to prevent him from advancing any further on the track of his thinking. Then with her elbow, she clipped his nose hard enough to hurt like a bitch. The instant he pulled his hand out from between her legs to check the injury to his nose. Bianca took the opportunity to spin in her seat, lift her foot and with all her pissed off at life attitude she kicked out, hitting Johnathon square in the chest. The umbrella scraped the side of the car as he fell backward landing on his ass in a puddle of mud.

"Schmuck!" Bianca growled in his general direction as she pulled the door closed and locked it from the inside. Taking a deep breath, she put the key into the ignition and started the engine. Exhaling she threw the car into gear and spun the wheels as she left the church parking lot. She drove back to her grandmother's house on Mulberry Lane and parked in the driveway. Getting out of the car she walked up the path to the front door and after closing it behind her she finally allowed herself to feel the grief of never being able to have one of her grandma's hugs ever again. She tossed her bag onto the entryway table along with her keys.

As she walked past the living room a

glimmer of light from the vestibule bounced off of something sitting on the highest shelf. Temporarily ignoring it, she walked towards the kitchen to find a glass and the bottle of rum that her grandmother always kept hidden for making her Christmas cakes every year, even though she herself never actually ate them. Walking by the dining room table she stopped and held her breath, turning her head to look at the table itself. At one end was the bottle of the infamous imported rum that her grandmother used for her damn delicious Christmas cakes and puddings. Next to the bottle of Bundaberg Rum was a glass and what looked like an envelope. Releasing her held breath, she rounded the table to the other side where she could see things from a different angle.

"What the fuck are you playing at Grandma Grey?" Bianca asked as her eyes targeted her name written in her grandmother's handwriting on the front of the letter leaning up against the bottle and glass. Pulling the chair out from the table she sat down and placed the envelope face down while she picked up the bottle and un-screwed the cap. Waving the bottle under her nose she closed her eyes and allowed the memories of her grandmother to hold her warmly in their embrace. She could smell the raw Christmas cake dough with all its fruit, nuts, spices and cherries as they soaked up the ample dousing of that delicious rum. Tears filled Bianca's closed eyes and as she blinked them open they slowly trickled down her cheeks. She brushed them away with her free hand while tipping the bottle to pour a hefty helping into the glass tumbler on the table. Returning the bottle to the table she picked up the glass and swirled the amber liquid before raising the glass above her head in a silent toast to her grandmother. "Gods speed," she whispered then she put the glass to her lips and drank down half the contents. "Holy shit!" she choked as the burn in the back of her throat took her breath away and a different sort of tears filled her eyes. It was nothing like eating the rum sodden cake mix when her grandmother wasn't looking, she smiled, then chuckled at the memory.

"Alright if you insist on doing this, then we are going to do it in comfort at least," Bianca spoke as if her grandmother was standing in the room beside her. She pushed herself to her feet and picked up the bottle, the glass and the letter then walked into the living room. Placing the bottle on the coffee table she emptied the contents of the glass and then put it down too. Swallowing this time didn't burn as bad as the first time and she contemplated refilling the glass. Tapping the unopened envelope against her open palm she wondered if she really wanted to do this right now. "Better now than when I'm three sheets to the breeze." She rolled her eyes and flopped down into the armchair lifting her feet to rest on the corner of the coffee table.

Tearing the corner, she slid her finger in to rip the letter open and retrieved the piece of paper inside. Unfolding it to see her grandmothers writing was as perfect as it had ever been, and Bianca wondered how long ago it had been that the letter was written. She inspected it for a date and found nothing to indicate how recently it had been composed. Bianca rubbed her temple as she started to read.

MY DARLING BIANCA,

If you are reading this then it means I'm dead, well isn't that a kick in the guts. I had hoped to be around to watch you walk down the aisle to marry the man of your dreams. I would have loved to have met my great grandchildren but I guess I can't complain. I was blessed to have you with me even after we lost your mother and father. Alright enough of the sad stuff, I have a list of things I need you to do for me.

1. *Make this year's Christmas cakes for the police department, ambulance service and the fire brigade. I promised them and they are raffling them off to raise money for the children's hospital.*
2. *Under no circumstances is Mavis ever to get her hands on my peach cobbler recipe. I'd rather you burn it so that it is never likely to fall into the hands of the enemy. That bitch*

*was always bitter after I took first
place in the bake-off seven years ago.*

3. *Always remember wishes come in
   threes unless you wish for forever.
   Infinity will also do.*

4. *Always remember I love you and that
   even though I would love for you to
   return to Sunshine I will respect your
   wishes if you chose to leave.*

*Take care of my most prized possession – the
teapot is on the top shelf in the living room, be
careful not to drop it as it is more delicate than
it appears.*

Love Grandma Grey.

Bianca was smiling as she re-folded the
piece of paper and slipped it back into the
damaged envelope for safe keeping. Dropping her feet to the carpet she stood and
grabbed the bottle of rum, this time she
didn't bother with the formality of using the
glass and tipped the bottle to her lips. Then

she sidestepped the coffee table and headed straight to the Arabian teapot mentioned in the letter she'd just read. Biting her lip in trepidation, she reached up on her tip-toes to take ownership of her grandmother's most prized possession. Studying the intricate patterns adorning the creation, she turned it this way then that as she whispered to herself.

"I WISH I understood why Grandma Grey forbid me to touch you?"

BIANCA GASPED as the teapot heated and a cold steam began to flow out of the spout. She then choked on her gasp as a half-naked man appeared and demanded to know, "Who dares to summon Shibari?"

CHAPTER 3

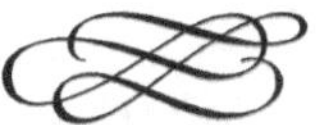

Bianca took a quick step backward, with her jaw dropping in astonishment. She blinked several times to establish if she was imagining things or not. "What the fuck did you do grandma?" Bianca turned in a circle expecting some kind of response from her recently departed family member, only, there was nothing and nobody there to respond. Well, that wasn't entirely true, there was a man without a shirt, wearing puffy pants, and funny slippers which curled up at the toes standing right in front of her. Bianca stood gobsmacked with her blank look on her face to match her stupefied mind. In all her thirty years of wisdom, she'd never witnessed anything quite like this.

Shibari impatiently waited for a response from the attractive female who he now looked up and down as if inspecting. The pallor of the woman's face gave him cause for concern and he softened his tone, "I am Shibari, who are you?" looking around he recognised his surroundings and prompted, "Where is Katrina Grey?" his eyes narrowed as he questioned his current circumstances.

Bianca reached out to touch the male's chest only she never made contact. Shibari blocked her movement by circling her wrist to hold her firmly in place. When she tried to free herself, he scowled with confusion. He called out, "Katrina, where are you? What's the meaning of this?"

"Hey Punjab! she can't hear you," Bianca replied. "At least I don't think she can hear you from where she is."

"Who is Punjab?" Shibari released his hold as though touching her had burnt him.

"I don't know who or what you are, or even where you came from but you need to leave." Bianca looked around the room as though trying to figure things out.

"You are the one who summoned me." Shibari put his hands on his hips and puffed up his chest.

"Then tell me how to send you back," Bianca asked.

"No!" Shibari responded noting that he had not had this sort of interaction with another person for many centuries even if the female was disrespectful.

"My grandmother passed away. She's gone in the physical sense of being alive." Bianca sighed, wondering if her vivid imagination was due to the lack of sleep and food or the Bundaberg Rum.

"Wait female! You say Katrina is dead? how did this happen?" Shibari asked as though not wanting to believe the young woman's words. "Is this some kind of trick?"

"Fuck my life," Bianca rambled to herself as she returned her focus to drinking more rum. Maybe if she drank more the voices in her head would go away. Knowing that she would only accomplish making herself violently ill if she continued to drink without eating something she headed for the kitchen.

"I'm feeling like one of your all-day breakfasts grandma, don't let me down in my time of need." Bianca opened the fridge relieved to find all the ingredients were available to make eggs, bacon, mushroom, sausages, and tomato. She cranked on the radio her grandmother kept on the bench for when she was cooking in the kitchen and changed the station to one she preferred.

Shibari stood puzzling over what to do, then when he heard the sound of music coming from Katrina's kitchen he walked to the doorway. Frowning he watched the female flutter around the kitchen opening cupboards and draws. The music wasn't loud enough to drown out the clattering of pans being placed on the stove or the click-click of the pilot light to ignite the gas and start cooking.

"What is your name?" Shibari asked, hoping that this time the woman would answer him.

"Jesus grandma did you roofie the rum?

Fine, they can lock me up for being as crazy as you were. Always talking to yourself when nobody else was around." She turned her attention to the food preparation and replied, "Bianca Ebony Grey and before you say, it's nice to meet you. No, it isn't. I'm having one of my not so great days. Now that I've told you my name, enlighten me, what is my delusional state of mind called."

Shibari smirked at the funny way the female spoke, "Shibari Khaleej at your service." He bowed his head in her direction even though she wasn't even looking at him.

"Well make yourself useful," Bianca pointed over to where the toaster and coffee maker was. "If you're not a figment of my emotionally challenged imagination, then you can at least make the toast and coffee. If you can't then I don't see the good of having you around or the logic in me making extra to feed you."

Shibari had not done any such menial tasks in many centuries if at all. He'd had servants to make his food before he'd been subjected to his impediment. Since then he'd not had any need for sustenance. He didn't even know if he could eat although the concept of investigating the idea was something he was keen to do. "I have no domestic training or knowledge but I am willing to give it a try." Shibari offered, moving from the doorway, following the direction of Bianca's pointed finger. On the bench were some silver coloured contraptions that he'd only ever seen from a distance. Those times had been when Katrina had made wishes for something special in every bite of her Christmas cakes and puddings. She'd always called him her secret ingredient, he smiled sadly thinking that he would never again grant her a wish. He pulled out a couple of slices of bread from the packet and sat them in the slots on top of the square box. Appraising the levers, he lowered them until they clicked into place then leaned over the top to check things out. As the heat rose from within the furnace inside the hot box he was satisfied that he managed to figure out the first request. Next, he inspected the coffee machine, following the steps on the side of the machine he filled it with water, added the coffee granules and a filter. As he waited to see what happened next, he felt proud of his accomplishments. While tending to the makings of coffee, the toast had popped up and he took it out and sat it on a plate near where Bianca was busily turning things over in the pan. Glancing at the toast deposited onto the plate Bianca's nose scrunched with a dislike for toast that wasn't buttered while still hot. "The toast needs butter on it before it gets stone cold." Seeing the baffled look on his face Bianca gave a loud sigh and moved past him to open the big cold box in the corner of the room. On the way, back she collected a butter knife from the drawer and within a minute the toast was buttered and the plate was placed in the middle of the kitchen table. "So, who did you announce yourself to be?" Bianca probed as she returned to finish off the items still in the pan.

"My name is Shibari," he answered cautiously.

"And you say I summoned you? How?"

"I will save that topic for after we have eaten. I do not wish... want, to return to my dwelling before I have a chance to get to know the world through your eyes."

"Okay, that was just a tad serial killer kind of creepy. You need to work on your delivery if you're going to hang around until I figure out how to send you back to where you came or better yet you leave of your own free will." She placed the plates of food on the kitchen table opposite each other and concluded her statement by returning to the cupboard for the salt and pepper, knife and forks. "Do you want any sauce?"

Shibari shook his head as he threw his leg over the chair to sit down, sniffing at the ample offerings covering his plate. "It smells good," he smiled.

"Yeah well, grandma Grey always insisted that I help in the kitchen, she said it would come in handy when I finally find a husband. She had this misguided conception that the way to a man's heart was through his stomach. I wasn't about to correct her on that one considering she wasn't far from the general area." Bianca chuckled to herself.

Shibari frowned, not really following all of the funny terms the female was speaking. In his time, a wife was not chosen for her ability to prepare food, they had servants for that task. As Bianca put a mouthful of food into her mouth and she used her finger to wipe a smudge of sauce from the corner of her lips, Shibari's mind traveled in the same direction. His eyes widened as the realisation hit of what she was saying, and he looked down at the material covering his lap. He had not felt stirrings of this nature in what felt like forever. They proceeded to eat their food in relative silence, if you could call it that. Especially when every time Shibari put food into his mouth he made disturbing noises like he was having multiple orgasms inside his mouth. He'd even started to squirm in his seat every so often before he leaned his back against the chair and closed his eyes in absolute abandoned awe of pleasure.

Bianca sat with her fork halfway between her plate and her mouth watching the entertainment package sitting opposite her. She was so hypnotised by the show that she put her fork down, crossed her arms and watched in amazement. Unable to stop herself she stood up and put both her hands flat on the table, one on either side of her plate and leaned over. The further she leaned, the more she figured it was better for her to see if what she suspected was true. Biting her bottom lip her vision cleared the opposing edge of the table giving her a clear line of sight to Shibari's lower half. "Oh my God, Grandma you old devil." She giggled, looking straight at the extremely well-tented frontage of Shibari's puffy pants.

Shibari barely noticed the shift of movement in the room, he was so caught up in the sensation of eating and the taste of blissful succulence on his tongue, that it took the sound of someone giggling to bring his attention back into focus. He brought his head back from its tilt and slowly opened his eyes to discover Bianca hovering before him with all of her focus bearing down on his throbbing manliness. He felt his cheeks heat and wasn't entirely sure which emotion it was attached to.

Firstly, he felt anger for her brazenness to make fun of him. Secondly, he felt no shame over his body's reaction to something that was not sexual in nature. And lastly, because he found Bianca so attractive that he wanted her as much, if not more than, he'd ever wanted for anything before in his extremely long existence. That confused him, and left him in a state of frustration.

Bianca's grin faltered as she realised that Shibari was now staring back at her with a not so happy look on his face. She coughed to clear her throat before speaking, "Coffee's ready." She turned on the ball of her foot and moved to where the coffee machine had announced the pot was done. Taking two cups from the wrack she poured them each a cup and returned to the table, only to find Shibari was no longer sitting at the table and the room was empty.

"Damn," Bianca sighed a curse. "And that Grandma Grey, is why I'm still single." She stated to nobody but herself and thin air. She never really understood men, they wanted to be looked at as though they were gods but then the instant they opened their mouths they made it quite apparent they were irrefutably human. Therefore, lay the fault line. Bianca would have been happy to find the right guy, settle down, and provide grandma Grey with a small number of bambinos to bounce on her knee and brag to all the major players in Sunshine. Only Bianca could never find anyone that fascinated her enough to hold a conversation with for more than five minutes before she was cringing at the idea of them laying a finger on her, let alone any other body parts.

She took a sip of her coffee before sitting it down on the table beside her plate, guilt prevented her from simply ignoring the missing elephant in the room. "Crap!" she muttered feeling bad for making the whole situation awkward. Leaving the kitchen, she searched the entire house only to find no sign of Shibari. "Well, that sucks out loud. I was just getting used to sharing oxygen with him." She confessed softly, not wanting to think about the hole in her chest. She shrugged, "Never mind, everyone leaves eventually." Bianca added, making her way back to the kitchen to finish her

5:00 PM breakfast and to clean up the mess from cooking it.

The house felt dreadfully empty as Bianca moved around unpacking her clothes from her suitcase and hanging them up. She was still undecided as to what to do about everything. Did she want to stay in Sunshine, the answer to that question was a double-sided blade. If she stayed would she ever meet a man that she could live happily ever after with? If she left for good, could she bear to think she was severing all ties with somewhere she'd always called home? Even though she no longer lived in Sunshine it was always home, it was the place she ran to when things weren't going the way she wanted them to. It was where she disappeared to when she needed to clear her head. Concluding that there was no solid resolution to her predicament at the moment, she chose to take a shower and get out of her black dress she'd worn to the funeral.

After getting into her pyjamas and slippers she returned to the kitchen to make herself a hot chocolate. Her grandmother had always told her that when she was away, the next best thing to one of her hugs was a hot chocolate, because it was like a deliciously warm hug in a mug. Bianca smiled as she heated the milk in the microwave on high for two minutes. After the ding, she removed the cup and added the drinking chocolate, stirring it gently as she remembered the many nights her grandmother had made it for her as a child. Especially on the nights when she missed her mum and dad. In the beginning, it had been almost every night, but as she got older it became less and less the reason behind having the hot chocolate.

CHAPTER 4

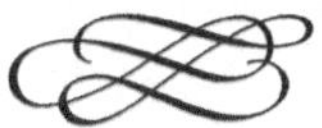

Shibari disintegrated in the living room and returned to the dreadful loneliness of his prison. It was only because of the mistress Katrina Grey did he now have a place that was somewhat bearable in living conditions. She had taken care of him over the many years, just as the mother he could no longer remember did. He could not be blamed for his lack of memories, after all, it had been many centuries that he'd spent inside the Arabian teapot before Professor Desmond Grey, Katrina's late husband had discovered the priceless artefact. It was while on a dig in the lower quadrant of Saudi Arabia near the Yemen border. He'd returned to his home in Sunshine and gifted the teapot to his wife Katrina to make up for the fact that she was unable go with him on the dig. She'd been at home looking after their granddaughter Bianca.

When he'd presented it to her, he had no idea how special the artefact was, and even though Katrina loved her husband dearly, she never told him about what she'd discovered while cleaning the precious piece the day after receiving it. Shibari was tired, almost insane from his own company and he'd developed a passionate dislike for the dark. Up until Katrina Grey began to make wishes on his behalf his world had been very bleak and now the thought of returning to that sort of existence threatened to break him. He lit the candle which was included in the supplies Katrina has provided for him and he wondered how long the other three would last. He mentally calculated it to be an approximate of two days and one night. He scratched his head, he needed figure out how to implement a plan to continue his existence in the manner he'd become accustomed to because of Katrina Grey's actions.

He flopped down on the pile of pillows in the middle of his room, trying not to remind himself that it was his prison in which there was no escaping.

The wish that Jasminda had given him those thousands of years ago was still something to be fulfilled. So, he thought if he could manipulate the situation he may be able to break the curse. He clicked his fingers, "That's it!"

* * *

BIANCA GRABBED the book she'd started reading a couple of nights ago and flopped down in the chair in the living room. She found her place in the bookmarked with her train ticket from the other day and started to read. It was the latest from her favourite paranormal romance author J. Thiele, so she easily sank into the storyline until she heard a knock at the front door. With an exasperated sigh, she returned the train ticket to the page she was on and sat the book down on the lounge. The knock turned into pounding and Bianca suddenly had a really bad feeling about opening the door to see who was on the other side. She'd told her grandmother many times she needed to get a peephole, but as usual, her grandmother never listened.

"Who's there?" she called out cautiously.

"Bianca, open the door darling," Gavin Richards replied.

"Oh for fuck sake," Bianca cursed under her breath. "I wish I had a man to prevent this shit from going down ever again." When a strong male arm wound around her waist and she was pulled back against a solid chest she felt her body come alive.

"Your wish is my pleasure, but a word of warning. That is wish number two, so be very careful what you wish for next." Shibari's lips brushed against Bianca's ear as his other hand settled on the deadbolt to unlock it. Swinging the door open Shibari raised his hand to the other man's chest, "Not so fast."

Bianca was struck mute, finally realising what the information in her grandmother's letter had said about making wishes. With an evil glimmer in the corner of her eye, she slipped her hand behind her back and cupped Shibari's manliness in the palm of her hand. Shibari dropped his forehead to Bianca's shoulder and cursed in his ancient tongue. He froze in fear as Bianca started to speak to the man standing on the stoop.

"You know what Gavin, I wish I had a thousand and one wishes. And if I did, you most definitely would not be one." Bianca closed the door in Gavin's face and re-locked it.

"Here's the deal. I need a man to show the town of Sunshine that I do not want or have need for one of theirs. In return, I will continue to do for you what my grandmother did. Does that sound cool to you?" Bianca pushed past Shibari then paused abruptly. Dropping her head, her chin rested on her chest, and she spewed the words out quickly before they made her physically ill. "Did you and my Grandmother ever – You know play hide the sausage?"

"That would be none of your business if

we had, but the answer is absolutely not. I looked at her as a replacement mother for one I lost a very long time ago." He smiled, then added. "However, you're too young to be seen in the same light, therefore I would be very much open to playing games such as hide the saus..."

"Stop right there! There will be no noodling or caboodling of any kind." Bianca added knowing all too well that if fronted with the opportunity, she would most definitely jump at it like an Olympic pole-vaulter. She shook her head knowing she was very interested at the thought of bumping slippery bits with the magic man. "Wait, what are you anyway?"

"I am a genie, and I have been trapped in the teapot for many centuries."

"Why?" Bianca asked curiously. "And by whom?"

"By King Mohammad bin Al Saud's sorcerer Mustafa, for refusing to marry the king's daughter."

"Wow sucks to be you. Is there no way for you to escape?"

Shibari lowered and shook his head

slowly in acceptance not wanting to talk about it any further, at least not if he was to succeed in winning the heart of the female standing before him along with his freedom. He refused to jinx himself, after all, he had one thousand and one wishes to grant to the fire-breathing female as part of the deal, his lips tilted up at the corners as Bianca spun around and stormed back to where she'd left her hot chocolate and book on the couch. Picking up the cup she downed the last of her drink, then kicking back she opened her book to where her marker was. Just as she was about to start reading Shibari plopped himself down on the couch beside her.

"If we are going to convince the town of Sunshine that we are more than strangers, and in fact that we are indeed seeing each other romantically, then we should perhaps know something about each other first." Shibari pointed out folding his arms across his muscular chest to prevent himself from being overly forward and openly touching Bianca.

Bianca narrowed her eyes at the half-naked man with the charm of a snake, "What sort of things do you want to know?" she asked warily.

Shibari shrugged nonchalantly then prodded, "Maybe we should start with the simple thing, such as," he paused a moment while he considered his options, then blurted. "your favourite colour?"

They sat talking for the next three hours getting to know each other and were quite surprised to find out that they had many more things in common than either of them could have imagined. Well at least they would have if they had been from the same era. Shibari admitted that he was curious about the world outside of Katrina Grey's house.

Bianca considered the information briefly then decided to show Shibari what was outside. "Come on!" She encouraged him to get up from where he sat. "I'll take you for a drive, but you have to put some clothes on. You can't go out wearing that." She pointed at his ballooned pants.

"What should I wear? I have no concept

of what is acceptable attire in the modern world."

"I wish you were wearing blue denim jeans and a grey t-shirt, just like what Gavin had on earlier."

Shibari smiled, "Your wish is my command." He clapped his hands three times and was suddenly dressed in the clothing that was wished for. He tugged at the back of his pants, not fond of the hugging and grabbing sensation around areas that were usually free of such confines. He then pulled at the neckline of the t-shirt feeling as though it were choking him. Everything was just painstakingly tight, especially around the front of his pants. When he took a couple of steps he thought he was being subjected to some sort of medieval type of torture. Three more steps and he was tripping over his own feet in frustration.

Bianca stood watching sympathetically as Shibari struggled to become accustomed to his attire and she felt a smidgen of guilt knowing that she'd neglected to include underwear. Judging from Shibari's reaction though, he was no longer the commando type, she smirked. Making a mental note to take pity on the genie next time, she shrugged her shoulders and headed out the door wearing her pyjamas and slippers. She somehow managed to refrain from outright laughing as Shibari walked down the front steps as though his ass was chewing on a piece of gum. The girlish squeak broke her ability to maintain composure as he opened the door and sank into the passenger's seat.

The look of disgust on Shibari's face only made her laugh harder until her sides hurt. "I wish you could see yourself through my eyes."

Shibari's mouth dropped open in a hor-rified expression, "You can't be serious?" he huffed.

Bianca laughed so hard she was crying, and couldn't manage to put two words to-gether. "Bmhahaha! Stop! It hurts… ha! Oh my god I've never had this much fun." She wiped away her tears and smiled at Shibari, "Thank you."

Before she did something stupid like kiss the growing glow from his face, she started the engine and reversed out of the driveway.

She flicked on the lights and the road was swallowed by the wheels as they drove down the street. Not exactly knowing where they were going, Bianca just drove wanting to show Shibari everything she could. Ten minutes later they pulled into an empty spot on top of Sunshine Hill. Bianca hadn't been up there since her senior year, she used to like parking up on top of the hill overlooking the town of Sunshine with all the night lights shining brightly, it was a stunning sight. Even ten years later, and with a population boom in the area, it took her breath away even more. They sat in relative silence until the sound of another vehicle drew their attention. Relief washed over Bianca when she saw the sheriffs truck pull up next to them, however, that was a short-lived reprieve when she saw Tucker climb out of the driver's side and tapped on her window.

"License and registration?"

Bianca cursed as she leaned over to

reach the glovebox, "Fuck! I wish I'd thought to grab my purse."

"Your wish is my command," Shibari tapped his knee three times with two fingers. When Bianca opened the glove compartment she found her purse and the registration papers inside. "I could kiss you," She said before turning to face Tucker. He'd always been a complete prick after she'd turned him down for the senior prom. He simply wasn't her type, and no amount of flowers and chocolates was ever likely to change that. He was never the same towards her after that.

Her grandmother was pretty sure it was him that had toilet papered their house that night but there was no way to prove it since his friends had all alibied him elsewhere.

They'd all claimed to be skinny dipping at Dan's place until three in the morning then they'd crashed in the guesthouse.

"Well if it isn't Bianca Ebony Grey." Tucker spat her name as though it were something toxic in his mouth that he was trying to spit out. 'Asshole', Bianca thought as she clenched her fist tightly to stop herself from saying anything that could be mis-construed by the sheriff.

"How long do you plan on being in town?" Tucker asked looking at the paper-work for the registration.

"I haven't decided yet Sheriff Tucker. I guess it depends on whether my fiancé and I decide to settle down in Sunshine and create a family here. It's what Grandma Grey always wanted. What do you think honey?" Bianca turned to look at Shibari, "Darling don't you wish we could settle down and make Sunshine our new home?"

Shibari knew Bianca had no idea that what she was saying was exactly what he had hoped for, wished for from the beginning. He narrowed his eyes at her and made a mental note to take this up with her at a later time when they didn't have an un-wanted observer.

"I'm really starting to have a good feeling about this place. I've heard a lot about it but now that I'm seeing it for myself I have to say, I think you're right sweetheart, I could see us starting a family here." Shibari played his part, placing his arm around the back of

Bianca's seat and his other hand on her knee as he leaned over to speak to the officer of the law. Tucker was such an asshole that he didn't even acknowledge that Shibari had spoken.

"Maybe we should catch up for coffee while you're here for your grandmother's funeral." He made to pass the registration and driver's license back to Bianca, only to drop the license on the ground. Bianca went to open the door to pick it up as the sheriff leaned down to retrieve it and was rewarded by a car door to the side of his head. If that wasn't enough he fell back into a puddle left behind after the rainstorm earlier that afternoon.

Bianca leaned down and picked up her license and then slammed the door shut again handing her quarry to Shibari for safe keeping. With trepidation, she turned around to look out the window at Sheriff Tucker.

"I'll just be on my way then sheriff," Bianca explained starting up the engine, she put the car in reverse and slowly turned the car around and headed back towards home.

On the way, she figured, 'when in Rome' and pulled into the local burger joint with a drive-thru window. Placing an order, she doubled everything and paid for it before moving to the next window. Picking up the order from the attendant at the second window they drove the rest of the way home.

They finished up their food in the lounge room while laughing about the sheriff's mishaps. Bianca hoped that would be the last she saw of Sheriff Tucker. Regardless she needed someone to talk to and the only person around was Shibari.

"I'm trying to figure out what to do," Bianca tried to explain. "The house is paid for in full and grandma would have left that to me in her last will and testament. I went to college to get my degree in arts and literature. I can work from pretty much anywhere I choose to set up. I have a solid clientele who send me proofs and I return them overnight. If I sell this place I may not get enough for it to buy something anywhere else." Bianca looked at Shibari, "I'm talking myself into staying here aren't I."

Shibari lifted his hand and cupped the side of Bianca's face. He ran his thumb over her lower lip then asked, "Would staying here with me be so bad?"

When she tried to find the words to answer her mouth opened and Shibari slipped his thumb between her lips as he leaned in to close the distance between them. His lips brushed against hers stealing her thoughts of any answer away. As she melted into his hold, his tongue slid into her mouth and incited a dance of passion with Bianca's tongue. The more he kissed her the more she wanted him to kiss her. Bianca wanted to get lost in the moment, to forget everything except the here and now.

Her grandmother had always said to live for the now, worry about the rest later. Well, it was time that Bianca started living.

CHAPTER 5

Bianca's phone started to beep with emails making her abandon their little let's get to know you session. With a sigh, she extricated herself from Shibari's hold, noting that it had felt just right. It wasn't too gentle to be wishy-washy and it wasn't too firm to be considered lukewarm. The minute she moved away from him she actually missed his comfort and warmth. As she checked her messages containing several documents that required proofreading before the morning she wished she could just, pausing that thought she looked over her shoulder at Shibari, who even though he still sat on the couch watching her, his eyes were still hungry with desire. "Fuck it!" She muttered, "I wish I didn't have to work tonight because it was already perfectly finished and returned to my client's ready for their new day of business." She gave Shibari a one-sided cheeky smile then winked at him. "That would mean we could get back to our previous topic of conversation."

Shibari clapped his hands together as fast as a hummingbird's wings, "Your wish is my command."

As quickly as Bianca's inbox had filled with requests they were replied to with the work completed with a hundred percent accuracy. Bianca yawned with exhaustion from having one of the longest days of her life. "I'm wrecked, I need to get some sleep if I'm going to handle the people of Sunshine in the morning without telling them all to fuck off," she laughed thinking about what she'd said to Mavis Peacock and Sonia Castle. Those women knew no shame, they had gone out of their way to tarnish her grandmother's good name. Sonia made scones that were like brick cakes and Mavis used packet cakes, thinking nobody would ever notice. She still found it unbelievable, when she recalled the condescending language that flew out of her grandmother's mouth the day Mavis was discovered buying three packets of absolutely chocolate brownies. On entering the competition area, Bianca's grandmother's eyes had all but bugged out of her skull when they both spied the tier of brownies with Mavis' name on the card in front of the plate. That was when all hell broke loose, Katrina Grey had walked straight up to Mavis, who was standing near her produce looking down her nose at the other people as they presented their baked goods for the bake-off.

Bianca's grandmother snapped her fingers at Bianca who had then stepped forward to place her mobile phone on her grandmother's upturned palm.

"Withdraw your fraudulent brownies or I will release the evidence to show that they were made from a packet mix, not from scratch. Most definitely not from a home-made recipe."

"I'd like to think you wouldn't do that, after all, it is for a good cause." Mavis gasped in horror at being discovered as a cheat.

"Oh, Mavis quit hiding up Reverend Bishop's ass of ill intent, the pervert is just shy of being a pedophile."

"You don't know that," she spat, trying to pull Katrina away from where others were congregating and out of earshot.

"Then you tell me why he was caught with the Sunday school teacher who is young enough to be his granddaughter at twenty-five?"

"That's a lie," Mavis accused just as the Reverend and the young church-going female entered the room. Mavis almost choked when the Reverend's hand tucked his shirt back into his pants and the young lady in question tried to tidy her hair and fix her lipstick. Katrina blatantly laughed in Mavis' face as her point was hammered home balls deep in the mouth of bimbo's. "You're vulgar Katrina Grey."

"Maybe, but at least I'm not a cheat."

Bianca wondered how every one of Sunshine was going to react when they found out that all their dirty little secrets were going to be published in a tell-all novel that her grandmother had been working on for the past eighteen months or more.

She knew she was mentally stalling, but she wasn't exactly sure of what she wanted to happen between her and Shibari. Did she want to go slow and get to know him first, or did she want to go hard and fast without limits? She closed her eyes and whispered, "I want it all."

"Then all you have to do is wish for it and it will be so." Shibari coaxed, stepping up behind Bianca to kiss the back of her neck.

"But if this is going to work then it can't be because of wishes or magic." She said breathlessly as his lips brushed her ear and then the sensitive spot just below.

"I will remind you of your words when I take you to the edge of ecstasy and you are begging to come."

"Talk is cheap, put your mouth where the money is." She directed him wrapping her hand up behind his head, as he cupped the front of her taking the weight of her breasts into his hands. Bianca leaned back against him, "I haven't done this in a while," She admitted.

Shibari laughed, "Me either." He hoped he did not make a fool of himself, his desire to pleasure Bianca was so strong, that he could punch holes in stonewalls with his cock, only the throbbing need was painful enough already to almost take him to his knees.

Bianca wasn't sure how, but one moment they were standing with her back to his chest and the next they were on a bed of cushions...naked. With a quick glimpse around she knew for sure they were not anywhere she'd ever been before.

"Please allow me to welcome you to my home?" Shibari humbly asked Bianca.

Licking her lips nervously Bianca nodded her head. She'd had lovers before, well no she'd had one night stands more than once. She just never found any of them interesting enough or good enough to double dip. But this was a whole new ball game to her.

Shibari moved slowly, building the anticipation of what was happening between them. His heart was thumping in his chest and he felt it all the way down to the tip of his shaft. He came down over the top of Bianca but held his body weight apart from hers. He licked her top lip as though it were a delicacy then sucked it between his own lips. Shibari then hypnotized her with his kisses into a fevered pitch of pleas for more.

It was as though Shibari was setting her on fire and the passion and desire ignited deep within her were aching to be released. As he lowered down her body to take first one needy nipple into his hot wet mouth, Bianca arched her back offering herself up to him completely. He teased her with his teeth and his tongue until he was sure that her pussy was as hot and wet as his mouth was on her nipples. Bianca squirmed her ass cheeks on the mound of pillows as Shibari trailed his kisses down her body. His teeth grazed her hip as he tantalized her with his prowess he nibbled his way down between her thighs before lifting his head to inspect his rewards. Bianca was bare down there and she knew from the way it felt when he lifted one leg over his shoulder and then the other that she was really wet. Before he had opened her up to him, her pussy lips had been slippery against each other. Her body ached to be filled and she wasn't sure how much more she could take. It had been way too long since she'd pleasured herself and besides it had never felt this fucking awesome before.

With her pussy opened up to him like a flower ready for the picking, Shibari blew out the breath he'd been holding. He'd be lucky if he didn't cum all over the cushions, he chastised himself trying not to rub his lower half of his body against the fabric. Attempting to distract himself from his own need he opened his mouth and covered the swollen nub at the apex of Bianca's pussy. He ran his tongue around and around several times then gave the protruding tip a little flick. He repeated his motions over and over, the more he did it the louder Bianca cried out with pleasure.

When he felt her desperation for satisfaction, he penetrated her tight snatch with two fingers. Slowly he stretched her convulsing muscles until he was knuckles deep inside of her. Eager to blow her mind and body, he curled his fingers upwards to find that special spot and at the same time he latched onto her engorged clit and sucked then released, then sucked again.

Bianca screamed as her body fractured into a million pieces of rapture. Her pleasure so intense her entire body was engulfed with electrical sparks. "Fuck yessssss!"

Before her orgasm had a chance to conclude, Shibari moved back up her body. "Look at me, Bianca. I want you to see what you do to me as I take you." Bianca followed his instructions still riding out the ebb and flow of her climax. Shibari aligned the head of his cock with her entrance then as he pushed into her in one swift thrust they both groaned from the added stimulation. Without further ado, Shibari pulled back then again buried his thickness to the hilt. "Wrap your legs around me, princess," he instructed Bianca. The change of the angle on the forward momentum had them both seeing stars and fireworks. Shibari quickly pulled out and flipped Bianca over, lifting her up by her hips he drove himself into her deeply over and over again. Bianca felt the need to come again growing like wildfire and she spread her legs further and lowered her fingertips to where they were joined. Collecting her own slippery juices, she circled her sensitive clit while pushing back to meet every inward stroke from Shibari. Finally, Bianca's legs shook and her toes curled as she came so hard she was on the verge of blacking out.

Shibari's roar of release echoed around them as his cock erupted with his hot seed in the depths of Bianca quivering pussy. He was not able to hold both of them up any longer as he gave one final plunge into her welcoming warmth and they collapsed onto the pile of pillows breathing heavily.

Shibari turned his head to look at Bianca only to find she was already asleep. He eased out of her body gently and then pulled her back into his arms encompassing her with his awe for his blessings. He knew he probably shouldn't, but he wished he could keep her.

Shibari and Bianca slept soundly until

movement woke Shibari. He covered Bianca's mouth with his hand then whispered into her ear, "Princess you need to wake up."

Bianca's eyes flashed open and she was instantly aware of Shibari's concern. They were moving it was a strange rock and roll to their entire world. "What's happening?" Bianca asked Shibari hoping that he had the answer.

"I don't know but it can't be good. If we are moving then it means someone has stolen the Arabian teapot," Shibari admitted.

"Oh no they didn't," Bianca bolstered her courage. "I haven't just found you to have you taken away from me. I need to know if we are still inside my grandmother's house." She kissed him quickly then spoke just as fast, "I wish I was in the bathroom of my grandma's house."

The sadness in Shibari's voice was so thick it could have been sliced with a knife. "Please we don't have much time," Bianca placed her hand on his face. "I will find you, I promise. And I also wish that you didn't have to grant any wishes for anyone else except me."

Shibari smiled knowing that Bianca meant every word she said, he bowed his head. "My Princess, your wish is my command." He clapped three times and Bianca no longer stood inside the Arabian teapot but in the shower cubicle within the bathroom of her grandmother's house.

Throwing the glass door open she grabbed a towel from the cupboard and wrapping it around her midsection she raced out of the bathroom. Checking each room one at a time there was no sign of the Arabian teapot and there was no evidence to indicate who had taken it.

Bianca sank to her knees on the floor and buried her face in her hands. For a few minutes, she thought she was actually going to cry, but then pissed off felt better. Who would dare to enter her grandmothers home? What kind of scum sucking fuck nugget would steal from a dead person? The list of people who came to mind was shorter than she thought, but Mavis Peacock and Sonia Castles were both at the top of that list.

Bianca stormed into the bathroom and

pulled her hair into a ponytail. Dropping the towel to the floor she used the toilet and then cleaned up the remnants of Shibari's sexual impact. Leaving the bathroom, she walked to her bedroom and found a set of clothes to wear suitable for kicking old lady asses. While getting dressed she muttered to herself, "Fucking old bitches give old people a bad name."

Tying her shoelaces, she jogged to the front door, collected her car keys and rushed out the door, only to slam straight into the bulky body of Sheriff Tucker. "Fuck!"

"Profanity is not becoming of you Bianca," Tucker said.

"Neither is being a stalker Tucker, so fuck you." Bianca roused trying to get past him.

"Not so fast little miss, you assaulted an officer of the law last night."

"And I'll do it again if you don't get your hands off me right this minute. Is Suzie's granddaddy still the judge?" She smiled as he released the hold he had on her upper arm. "Tucker one day you're going to figure out that the reason people don't like you, is not because of the uniform. It's because you're a knob jockey blowhard." Bianca explained as she raced over to her car. Flipping Sheriff Tucker the bird she revved the engine and then reversed out of the driveway.

The first place she stopped was at Mavis Peacock's on Maple Lane, as she stopped her car she spied Mavis and Sonia sitting on the front porch drinking tea and eating biscuits. "Okay so it can't have been either of those old moles, they drive slower than two turtles fucking."

She crossed them off her list and moved on to the next name in her hater's club. Weeding out four more people who were exactly where they were supposed to be at this time was disheartening. "Shibari where the fuck are you?" she wondered aloud after feeling as though she were chasing ghosts and myths in circles.

Bianca returned to her grandmother's house, walking into the living room she sat down in the single armchair looking at the place on the shelf where the Arabian teapot stood for more years than Bianca could count using both the fingers on her hands or all of her toes. Knowing her grandmother there was no possibility that she would have openly displayed the teapot. Which left Bianca with the conclusion that it had to be someone who her grandmother had trusted even if it were misguided.

Bianca mentally tore off the top sheet of a notepad in her mind and stared at a blank page for a number of minutes. Taking a calming breath as nobody fitting the bill came to mind immediately, she tore off another piece of paper and scrunched it up tossing it over her shoulder. That was when she sat up and started looking for her grandmother's letter. She fell to her knees and looked under the coffee table, she crawled to the three-seater lounge and shoved it back. Nothing but carpet, everywhere she looked, "Son of a bitch, motherfucker!" Whoever had taken the teapot had also taken the only real evidence to prove that her grandmother had willed her the teapot as part of her inheritance.

Bianca considered the sanctity of the funeral package and the man who'd helped arrange it, Simon something. Then there would be the attorney gran had used, he would be privy to how that letter got onto the table with the bottle of rum and a glass after she'd arrived home from the funeral that first day. She paced back and forth trying to remember who else could possibly have gained access to the place.

Bianca suddenly saw a flash of memory and realized there was another possibility - Franklyn Moon. A skerrick of doubt flittered through her mind, after all, Franklyn had worshipped the ground that her grandmother had walked on. It was unrealistic to believe that he would take something that had been given with love from her grandfather to her grandmother. Bianca knew that if her grandmother never once divulged the specialty of the teapot to her husband, then there was no way she would have told Franklyn Moon either.

CHAPTER 6

Franklyn Moon sat in the old shed out the back of his house. He ran his hand through his mussed-up hair and he dug into his pocket for his packet of tobacco. On the top of an old timber crate sat the Arabian teapot. Franklyn pulled out a paper and a scrunch of tobacco from his pouch. He rolled it with cranky fingers into a messy cigarette, pinching the tips off either end he tossed the crumbs back into the pouch. Licking his lips, he put one end into his mouth and lit it with the flick of a match. Taking a long drag he inhaled the smoke deep into his lungs while pondering how to make the Arabian teapot work.

Franklyn knew there was something about the way Katrina refused to talk about the teapot using the excuse that it was a gift from her long-dead husband only Franklyn could always tell that she was lying. There was something very special inside the teapot except he couldn't figure out how to open it. It was where Katrina hid her stash of money, he'd seen her pull large amounts of money from it when she thought he wasn't looking. He'd feigned sleeping in the chair after they'd watched a movie together one night and Katrina stood carefully not to disturb him. Then she'd tiptoed over to the top shelf to retrieve the teapot, lifting it down she whispered something into it and then tugged wads of cash from inside it.

Franklyn needed that money now more than ever, since he'd gotten in over his head with Tucker and the boys playing poker. Katrina was always there to bail him out whenever he'd been in a bind, but now that she was dead, he had no other option than to take the teapot with the money she had saved up inside. Only the damn lid was not coming off, it would not open. No matter how many times he tugged, pulled, hit it with a hammer or tried to pry it open with a knife it would not budge. Every ounce of strength he had in his withered old body was zapped. Now he leaned back on the workbench considering what other options he had. His eyes flicked from the grinder to the ox-torch and back to the grinder. If he weren't so damn desperate to get his hands on the money inside, he would have been embarrassed for treating an artefact in such a manner that would have Tutankhamen turning over in his tomb. He pulled Katrina's letter from his top pocket and felt only a little bit of guilt for Bianca. He'd have to burn the letter leaving the Arabian teapot to her, but even if he couldn't open the bloody thing, he had a buyer lined up to buy it for enough to cover his debt and more. He wiped his hand over his whiskered chin, "Why couldn't you have just married me, Katrina." Franklyn bellowed in frustration.

Bianca parked out the front of Franklyn Moons shitty little cottage and was about to walk up to the front door when she heard his muffled voice yelling from somewhere out the back. Following the sound, Bianca heard him ask, "Why couldn't you have just married me, Katrina." She momentarily felt guilty for suspecting the old guy until he finished the sentence. "It all would have been mine if you had."

Rage filled Bianca's heart and she stormed the shoddy door of the shed, kicking it in. "You slimy old bastard! and to think I thought you were grieving the loss of my grandmother when all you really wanted was her money, her land, and her belongings." Bianca snatched up the Arabian teapot from where it sat. She then kicked the old wooden crate into Franklyn's path as he tried to stop her from taking possession of it again.

He lifted the letter and threatened to set fire to it, "I'll turn it to ashes if you don't give it back."

Bianca shook her head, "No Franklyn. You're that stupid kind of evil that would still set fire to it even if I did give this back."

"Just give me the money inside it and I'll let you leave." Franklyn bargained, thinking that maybe Katrina had passed on the secrets of how to open it to her beloved granddaughter.

"So, you don't know how to make it work?" Bianca gloated, "You need to keep your distance, sit over there and don't say a word."

Thinking he was about to know all of Katrina's secrets he did as he was told. Eagerly perched on a second crate he watched as Bianca lovingly rubbed her fingers along the side of the Arabian teapot. "I wish Franklyn Moon was locked up in Sunshine Sanatorium for telling stories about genie's in bottles and making wishes."

Franklyn was completely focused on the steam pouring from within the teapot, out of the spout and as it hit the floor of the shed it solidified into the shape of a man. Shibari crossed his arms and bowed to Bianca. "If that is your wish, then it is my command." Shibari clapped his hands thrice and Frankly was no longer sitting on the timber box in his garage. He was inside a white padded room inside the section known as sector H. It was the area that housed the delusional schizophrenics, and

Franklyn screamed until his throat was hoarse and his head hurt. "Let me out of here! I tell you it was the genie who put me here. I want to go home."

* * *

BIANCA DROVE them home to her Grandmother's house and as they walked up the front steps to go inside Bianca watched the way Shibari's perky ass filled out the denim jeans and couldn't help wishing he didn't have them on. Spontaneously as Shibari turned around to face Bianca on the top step his clothes vanished.

"Oh my God. What are you doing?" She asked frantically looking around. "Get inside, before someone sees you." She laughed trying to keep a straight face while berating him, knowing full well it was her that had wished it in the first place.

"I like this thing that we do," Shibari told Bianca.

"What? fight?" she laughed.

Shibari cornered her in the kitchen, "No

he chuckled, it is not fighting my princess. What we do is called foreplay."

He lifted her up over his shoulder and carried her into the bedroom where he gently laid her down.

Shibari tenderly kissed her to thank her for coming to find him. She had kept her word and he would honour her for it. Bianca had other ideas. Shibari had turned her into a howling bundle of goo and she thought it only fair and just to return the favour now that they were in her room inside her grandmother's house. Sitting up, she pushed Shibari to stand in front of her. She forced him to take a step back in order to have some room to move. Then ever so slowly, she lifted his shirt up and over his abs, sliding up his ribs, past his chest and over his head. She kissed him with passion, excitement and the thrill of adventure. She'd never wanted to get to know all the little hot spots on a man before. However, when it came to Shibari she wanted it all, she wished she could have him forever. In between kisses, her words were soft and breathless, but Shibari heard them all the same and his heart raced as the adrenaline coursed through his body like a drug. He clucked his tongue and he replied in muffled words as his breath was taken away. Bianca dropped to her knees and circled his cock with her tight fist. Sticking her tongue out towards her chin, she licked the visible half of his throbbing shaft from the top of her hand to the crown. Then running her tongue around the crest as though it were an ice-cream cone she teased him until his hands shook and his legs trembled. He spoke in his ancient tongue of him belonging to her and she to him. Bianca's free hand curved around his hip and encouraged him to flex his thrust. She maintained complete composure as he lost control, as the tingle started in the small of his back he knew he would not be able to last much longer.

"Enough!" he ordered.

Bianca had read many books and always wondered if what the authors wrote were based on knowledge and experience. Eager to test her theory she placed her hand in between Shibari's thighs not once releasing him from her mouth. With her thumb and forefinger, she captured Shibari's balls. Then as she rolled her hand under gently, her index finger rested against his perineum. Not wanting to cause any pain she allowed him to slip briefly from her mouth as she explained what she was doing. "I want to apply a small amount of pressure here," she used her hand to show him. "It will stop you from coming and it will make your orgasm more intense when you do come."

Only because it seemed to be important to Bianca that she does this for him that he consented with a nod of his head. Bianca sucked him back into her warm wet mouth and resumed the long of succulent strokes in and out of her mouth.

As Bianca drew Shibari to the edge of madness she also stopped him from falling over the cliff. The pressure behind his balls was not unpleasant and he realised she was closing off the tubes that his seed travel through to make their release. The more intense the experience the more extreme the sensation. He had not planned on coming inside Bianca's mouth but when she could no longer maintain her hold on his balls she let go and allowed him to free flow into her throat. Shibari collapsed onto the bed physically, mentally and emotionally shaken.

Bianca covered him with the quilt knowing that her favourite authors of paranormal romance novels knew a thing or two about sex. Smiling to herself she climbed into bed beside him knowing there would be plenty of opportunities like this one in the future. They fell asleep in each other's arms and slept for ten hours straight.

Every day after that Bianca fell a bit more in love with Shibari and Shibari fell more in love with Bianca. She found it to be monumental amounts of fun in bringing Shibari into her world and he discovered that they liked a lot of the same things. Such as chocolate ice-cream, hot and horny sex, just to mention a couple, not necessarily in that order and most definitely together.

* * *

OVER THE NEXT THREE MONTHS, a number of odd events happened of which all of them were predicted in Katrina Grey's novel, *'Stick it Where the Sun Don't Shine.'* The inscription inside the cover was dedicated to all of her family for which Bianca thought was quite peculiar seeing as there had only been the two of them. Anyway, not to break the freakiness of things her grandmother seemed to know just about everything about everyone. Every dirty little secret was slammed in-between the covers of her grandma's novel. What appeared to make things reverberate like the ripples on a pond was that the headlines of the Sunshine News mirrored what Katrina Grey's book divulged to the general public. The headlines in the Sunshine News showed Sheriff Tucker being arrested for gross misconduct. That saw two days on the front page with full-colour photos to match as they hauled his ass off in the back of his own squad car. Apparently, it was discovered that he'd been screwing the Judge's assistant in order to raise his conviction rates.

* * *

ANDREW the new next-door neighbour to Grandma's house placed an add in the Sunshine News – Desperate and Dateless section and Simon answered the advertisement. They have been spending quite a bit of time together, although they are taking it slow. They planned to take it to the next level at the end of their fifth date.

Grandma Grey's book predicts they will be living together within three months.

* * *

GAVIN RICHARDS WAS TAKEN into custody for tax fraud. He'd been diluting the pension plans from Richard & Co for more than three years after taking over the company. He was also wanted by the Feds for money laundering for the mob.

* * *

MAVIS PEACOCK and Sofia Castles were taken into custody for being the ringleaders of a drug cartel. They'd been under surveillance for more than six months for making hash brownies even though they tried to tell the cops that it was Katrina Grey's secret recipe nobody seemed to believe them because one entire shelf in the pantry was full of Absolutely Chocolate Brownie packet mix.

* * *

FOUR YEARS LATER...

AND LAST BUT NOT LEAST, Grandma Grey's ashes were placed safely inside the Arabian teapot on the mantel in the living room. It was where everyone could appreciate the beauty of the artefact and it reminded them of how things began.

Shibari sat with his wife beside him, and his three-year-old daughter on his knee, Arabella yawned then asked her father, "Tell me a bedtime story daddy."

Shibari unable to refuse his little princess anything started his tale. "Once upon a time, long ago when tales of Alibaba and the Forty Thieves were bedtime stories and Scheherazade was titled Queen of 1001 tales in 1000 nights. There was a Prince who dared to wish for something more…"

Melissa Bell lives in Brisbane, Australia. She has loved to read since the age of twelve when she discovered 'To Kill A Mocking Bird', previous to reading this book she hated reading. With a couple of handfuls of years and thousands of books later she wanted to try writing.

When she is writing, she loves to listen to her favorite Australian bands - Birds of Tokyo and Karnivool.

She most recently made the USA Today Best Sellers List in October 2021 and has now set her sights on reaching the NY Times Best Sellers List.

She enjoys good food and good company when she's not trying to concentrate on what she's writing. She loves to laugh as laughter makes the world go round not money. Unfortunately laughter doesn't pay the bills unless you're a really well-known stand-up comedian. Which she is not. She is hoping that this is the start of an exciting adventure as a published Author, and that maybe something amazing will come of it. She would like to invite you all to join her on her journey.

Please keep an eye out for other books by Melissa Bell.

OTHER BOOKS BY MELISSA BELL

Dutiful Gods Series

Book #1 Destiny's Fate

Book #2 Taming Destruction

Book #3 Morpheus's Dream

Book #4 Defying Death

Five Brothers Series

Book#1 Houston
Book#2 Felan
Book#3 Tate
Book #4 Channon
Book #4.5 Lupe
Book #5 London
Brody and Blaez will be next in this series -
TBA

www.ingramcontent.com/pod-product-compliance
Lightning Source LLC
Chambersburg PA
CBHW051849130726
47987CB00002B/746